Amelie
the Seal
Fairy

To Tess Ruby Penman,
a very special friend of the fairies!

Special thanks
to Narinder Dhami

ISBN 978-0-545-27036-6

12 11 10 9 8 7 6   12 13 14 15 16/0

Printed in the U.S.A.   40

This edition first printing, March 2011

Amelie
the Seal
Fairy

by Daisy Meadows

SCHOLASTIC INC.

New York   Toronto   London   Auckland

Sydney   Mexico City   New Delhi   Hong Kong

With the magic conch shell at my side,
I'll rule the oceans far and wide!
But my foolish goblins have shattered the shell,
So now I cast my icy spell.

Seven shell fragments, be gone, I say,
To the human world to hide away,
Now the shell is gone, it's plain to see,
The oceans will never have harmony!

Contents

Magic Lantern

"Look at the lighthouse, Rachel!" Kirsty Tate exclaimed to her best friend, Rachel Walker. "Isn't it beautiful?"

Rachel shaded her eyes from the sun and gazed at the lighthouse. The tall, newly-painted red and white building stood proudly among the rocks at the harbor entrance. "It's very nice," Rachel agreed. "It looks so much better than it did before."

"Everyone in town helped raise the money to renovate the lighthouse and turn it into an artists' studio," Kirsty's gran explained. Kirsty and Rachel were spending their spring vacation with her in the coastal town of Leamouth. "There's been a lot of work going on since the last time you were here."

Rachel and
Kirsty glanced
at each other
and smiled. On
their last visit
to Leamouth,
they'd met Shannon the Ocean Fairy.
The girls had helped her to recover three
enchanted pearls that had been stolen by
Jack Frost and his goblins.

Now Rachel and Kirsty were in
the middle of another thrilling fairy
adventure! At the beginning of their
vacation, King Oberon and Queen
Titania had invited the girls to come
to the Fairyland Ocean Gala. It was
held on the beach just outside the Royal
Aquarium.

There, Rachel and Kirsty had seen

Shannon again, along with her friends, the seven Ocean Fairies: Ally the Dolphin Fairy, Amelie the Seal Fairy, Pia the Penguin Fairy, Tess the Sea Turtle Fairy, Stephanie the Starfish Fairy, Whitney the Whale Fairy, and Courtney the Clownfish Fairy.

They told the girls that the highlight of the Ocean Gala was always the moment when Shannon played the magic golden conch shell. It brought peace and order to the oceans of Fairyland and the human world each year.

But just as she was about to do that, Jack Frost had appeared and ordered his goblins to grab the golden conch shell. As the goblins argued with each other, the shell had fallen to the ground and shattered into seven shining pieces.

Immediately, a bolt of icy magic from Jack Frost's wand had sent the pieces whirling away into the human world. Rachel, Kirsty, and the fairies were horrified! They knew that without the golden conch shell, there would be chaos in oceans everywhere.

"Last time we were in Leamouth, Jack Frost was up to his old tricks," Kirsty whispered to Rachel, as her gran walked along the path to the lighthouse. "Now we're back again, and so is *he*! We have to find all the pieces of the conch shell, Rachel, so that it can be put back together again."

"Don't forget that the magic ocean creatures will be guarding the missing pieces," Rachel reminded her.

Luckily, Queen Titania had acted quickly after Jack Frost and his goblins had vanished. Inside the Royal Aquarium, she'd shown the girls the seven magic ocean creatures who belonged to the Ocean Fairies: a dolphin, a seal, a penguin, a turtle, a starfish, a whale, and a clownfish. All of them glittered with golden fairy magic. Then, with a wave of the queen's wand, the creatures had vanished. Queen

Titania's spell had sent them into the human world to guard the seven missing pieces of shell until Kirsty, Rachel, and the Ocean Fairies could find them and bring them back to Fairyland.

"Yes, but Jack Frost knows about Queen Titania's spell now, and he's sent his goblins out to look for the shell pieces, too," Kirsty pointed out anxiously.

"Well, we helped Ally and Echo the dolphin return the first piece to Fairyland, didn't we?" Rachel replied. "Now we just have to wait for the magic to come to us again!"

"Girls, come along," Kirsty's gran called. "I don't want to be late for my painting class."

Kirsty and Rachel ran to catch up with her. As they approached the lighthouse, they saw that a line of easels overlooking the ocean had been set up outside. There were people sitting at some of the easels, painting views of the water and the lighthouse. "Maybe you'd like to explore the lighthouse for a while, girls?" Gran suggested as she headed for an empty easel. "It's been renovated inside, too, and there are lots of paintings on display. Even the big old lantern right

at the top is working again. It's just for
show, though. Ships don't need it to tell
them where the shore is anymore."

Leaving Gran to unpack
her paints and brushes,
the girls wandered
over to the lighthouse.
The door was open,
and Rachel and
Kirsty went
inside.

"Let's climb right
up to the top," Rachel
suggested.

"Good idea,"
said Kirsty, heading
for the narrow spiral
staircase. The walls on either side of the

steps were hung
with watercolor
paintings, pencil
sketches, and
collages of
different views
of Leamouth.
The girls stopped
occasionally to
take closer looks.

"I can't believe
the big lantern
is working again,
can you?" Kirsty
asked as they
climbed higher.
"Last time we
were here, the

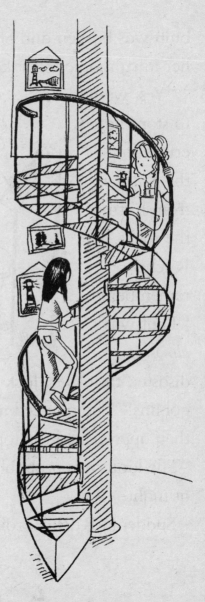

bulb was broken and Shannon had to use her fairy magic to make it light up."

"Yes, we had to stop that cruise ship, the *Seafarer*, from hitting the rocks," Rachel remembered. "That was *almost* a  disaster, thanks to Jack Frost and his goblins!" She glanced up the stairs as they approached the top of the lighthouse. "The lantern is probably only turned on at night—"

Suddenly Rachel broke off, her heart

pounding. They were almost at the top of
the stairs now and she
could see a
sparkling golden
glow ahead of
them, coming
from the lantern
room.

"What is it,
Rachel?" Kirsty asked curiously from
behind her.

"I can see a light coming from the
lantern!" Rachel declared.

"Why would the lantern be turned on?"
Kirsty asked, confused. "It's the middle of
the day."

"That glow *isn't* from a lightbulb,"
Rachel replied, "I think it's fairy magic!"

Breathless with anticipation, the two
girls ran up the last few steps and into the
room at the very top of the lighthouse.
Sure enough, the lantern was glowing
with a magical golden light.

"Look, Rachel!"
Kirsty cried, pointing
at the mirrors
surrounding the lantern.
"There are lots of
fairies!"

"But they all look
the *same*," Rachel said,
sounding confused.
Then she burst out
laughing. "Kirsty, it's
only *one* fairy!" Rachel explained.
"Those are just reflections."

The girls heard a tinkling little laugh, and a tiny fairy flitted out from inside the lantern. She had long brown hair with straight bangs, and she wore a patterned dress, gladiator sandals, and a chunky beaded bracelet on her wrist.

"It's me, girls," she cried, "Amelie the Seal Fairy!"

Conch Confusion

Smiling widely, Amelie flew over to Rachel and Kirsty.

"It's great to see you again, Amelie," said Rachel. "How are Ally and Echo the dolphin?"

"Echo's very glad to be back in the Fairyland Aquarium," Amelie replied, twirling her wand. "But she's lonely

because all the
other tanks are still
empty! I just have to
find Silky, my seal,
and the second
piece of shell."

"So what are you doing
here, Amelie?" asked Kirsty.

"I thought I might be able to spot Silky
from the top of the lighthouse," Amelie
explained. "And I did! He's with a pod of
seals at the farthest end of the shoreline."

"So the shell must be close by!" Rachel
exclaimed. "What are we waiting for?"

Amelie laughed. Hovering around
Kirsty and Rachel, she pointed her wand
at them. A misty cloud of sparkling fairy
magic swirled around the girls, lifting
them gently off their feet.

When the magic sparkles cleared,
Rachel and Kirsty opened their eyes.
They found themselves standing on a
large flat stone on a deserted outcrop
at the end of Leamouth beach. To their
amazement, they were surrounded by a
small group of sleek gray seals! One of the
seals had an adorable, furry white baby
nestled close to her side.

"I've never seen seals in Leamouth before," Kirsty said with delight.

"That's because they're not usually around here at all!" Amelie told her. "The missing golden conch shell is causing all kinds of chaos for ocean creatures."

"The seals *do* look very strange," Rachel pointed out. The seals were barking excitedly to each other and scooting around the rocks on their flippers. It seemed like they were searching for something.

"Do you see those pelicans on the beach over there?" Rachel continued, spotting two white birds with huge yellow bills. They were scooping up piles of shells with their enormous beaks as fast as they could, and dumping them on the rocks. "What are *they* doing? The only animal who's acting normally is that walrus asleep on the rocks—"

Suddenly Rachel broke off. She stared at the huge, heavy, brown walrus with long white tusks, sleeping in the sun.

ZZZZ . . .

"Now I'm really confused!" she exclaimed. "Pelicans and walruses don't live in Leamouth either, do they?"

Amelie shook her head. "No, these animals are far from home. It's all because of the lost golden conch shell," she explained. "You can see why we have to find the pieces and put it back together again!"

Kirsty gazed out over the ocean with a frown on her face.

"The missing shell might not be the only thing that's bothering the seals," she said anxiously. "Look!"

Rachel and Amelie turned and saw a row boat bobbing slowly toward the rocks where they were standing. The boat had a mast made out of a tree branch with a tattered flag flying from the top.

"There's a picture on the flag," Rachel
said. She squinted in the sunshine, trying
to make it out.

"I hope it doesn't have a skull and
crossbones on it," Kirsty joked.

Amelie shook her head. "It's much worse
than that, girls," she said solemnly. "It's a
picture of Jack Frost. Goblins ahoy!"

Pirates on the Prowl!

As the boat came a little closer, Rachel and Kirsty could see that Amelie was right. The flag fluttering in the breeze did have a picture of Jack Frost scowling darkly on it.

"How many goblins are there?" Kirsty asked, straining to see.

"Three, I think," Rachel replied. Then she smothered a giggle. "Look!" she whispered. "They're pretending to be pirates!"

The three goblins were dressed in pirate costumes. They wore baggy pants, floppy white shirts, and big leather boots. One had a pirate hat, one had a red and white spotted bandanna, and the third was wearing a black eye patch.

"Look at their boat!" Amelie exclaimed suddenly. "It's full of shells."

Rachel and Kirsty could see now that the boat was overflowing with hundreds of different shells.

The goblins were sorting carefully through the pale, shining piles of cream,

pink, and yellow shells, examining each
one carefully and then tossing it away in
disgust.

"They're looking for
the missing pieces of
the golden conch
shell!" Kirsty
guessed as a
goblin tipped
a bucket of
discarded shells
into the ocean.

"Well, they
obviously haven't found any *yet*," said
Amelie, looking relieved.

Rachel glanced around. There were
thousands of shells lying on the rocks and
the beach, plus huge piles in the goblins'
boat.

"Neither have we, though!" she pointed out, looking worried. "How will we ever find one piece of shell in all of these other shells?"

Kirsty nodded in agreement. "The golden conch shell has a magical shimmer," she said, "but all of these shells are sparkling in the sunshine!"

"Don't worry, girls," Amelie said, glancing at their downcast faces. "I know that Silky is around here somewhere. He'll help us find one of the missing pieces. I'll call him with my song. . . ."

Fluttering around Rachel and Kirsty, Amelie began to sing:

The oceans are special, everyone knows,
Feel the waves between your toes,
See the rainbow fish glide by,
Look a whale straight in the eye,
Watch the dolphins leap and play,
Swim with seals along the bay,
There's a beautiful world beneath the seas,
The oceans are special, everyone agrees!

At the sound of Amelie's sweet, soothing voice, the sea creatures around them grew still and calm. The seals lay down on the rocks, and the pelicans stopped scooping up shells.

ZZZZ . . .

Rachel glanced at the walrus, who was still sleeping peacefully. The next moment, she saw a seal's head pop up from behind the walrus's huge body. As the seal stared at them with bright eyes, Rachel saw a faint mist of golden sparkles around it.

"Silky!" Rachel exclaimed.

Amelie spun around and spotted her
seal. Silky bounded
out from
behind the
walrus and rushed
across the rocks toward her.

"Good boy, Silky!" Amelie laughed,
patting his head. "Now, where's the
missing piece of shell?"

Silky barked excitedly. Rolling over, he
pointed his flipper at the walrus, who was
still happily snoring away on the rocks.

Amelie turned to Rachel and Kirsty
with a frown.

"Girls," she announced, "Silky says
that the walrus is on top of the shell.
Somehow, we have to move that walrus!"

Wings and a Walrus

ZZZZ . . .

"Oh, no!" Rachel gasped.

"How can we get the walrus to move?" Kirsty wanted to know.

"We'll ask him very politely!" Amelie suggested. "Come on."

Rachel and Kirsty climbed over the rocks toward the sleeping walrus, while Amelie hovered just above him.

"Excuse me!" Amelie said, giving the

walrus a gentle tap with her wand.

The walrus snorted and sighed grumpily, but didn't open his eyes.

"Maybe we could all say it together," Kirsty suggested.

"On three, then," Amelie agreed. "One, two, three!"

"EXCUSE ME!" Rachel, Kirsty, and Amelie said loudly.

The walrus stirred a little. He wiggled his nose, yawned widely, and then sank back onto the rocks without opening his eyes. Seconds later, he was sound asleep again.

"This isn't working." Kirsty sighed.

"There's no way two girls and a fairy can move a walrus!" Rachel added, frustrated.

"Wait, I have an idea!" Amelie exclaimed. With a quick flick of her wrist, she sent a shower of magical sparkles from the tip of her wand straight toward Rachel and Kirsty. The girls began to shrink down to fairy-size. Just a few seconds later, they were flying up into the air to join Amelie. The paper-thin, shimmering wings on their backs glittered in the sunlight.

"Why did you turn us into fairies, Amelie?" Kirsty asked, looking very confused. "Now we're even smaller, and it'll be even harder to move the walrus!"

Amelie smiled. "Sometimes, all anyone needs is a little laughter," she replied mysteriously.

Kirsty and Rachel glanced at one another.

"OK, so the walrus *does* look pretty grumpy!" Rachel agreed. "But how will laughing help?"

"And how do you make a walrus laugh

 anyway?" Kirsty added. "By telling walrus jokes?"

Amelie burst out laughing herself. "No, you *tickle* it!" she explained. "And there's

nothing better for tickling than fairy
wings. Let's give it a try before the goblins
come to shore."

Amelie, Rachel, and Kirsty flew down
closer to the walrus. All three of them
began to flutter their wings against the
walrus's neck, tickling him gently. Silky
sat on some nearby rocks, in case they
needed help.

ZZZZ . . .

"Is it working?" Kirsty panted as she tickled away.

"Yes, he's opening his eyes!" Amelie cried. Silky barked encouragement and clapped his flippers. "Keep tickling, girls!" Amelie instructed. The walrus blinked, grunted a few times, and began to wiggle and shake. Then he opened his mouth and let out a loud bellow.

"He's laughing!" Amelie said.

Rachel and Kirsty couldn't help laughing themselves as the walrus wiggled a little more, rolling heavily from side to side.

As he rolled over and away from her, Kirsty caught a faint glimpse of a magical golden glow.

"There's definitely a piece of the golden conch shell under the walrus!" she told Rachel and Amelie excitedly. "We just need him to move a little more so we can grab it."

"More tickling, girls!" Amelie instructed.

Rachel and Kirsty's wings were getting tired, but they did as Amelie said. The walrus snorted and groaned with laughter. He began to roll around more and more!

"Just a little further!" Kirsty said eagerly, catching another glimpse of shimmering golden light.

Suddenly, a loud *BANG* made Amelie and the girls jump.

"What was *that*?" Rachel gasped, spinning around.

"It's the goblins!" Amelie cried, pointing to the ocean. "Look, they hit a rock and made a big hole in the side of their boat!"

The goblins had been so busy sorting through their shells that they hadn't been paying attention to where they were going. Their boat had smashed right into the rocks! Now the boat was filling up with water and starting to sink slowly beneath the waves.

"Help!" the goblins yelled, as they frantically tried to bail water out of the boat with wooden buckets. "HELP!"

Pupnapped!

"Come on, girls!" Amelie flew into the
air. "We have to help them!"

Leaving the walrus lying on the shell,
Rachel and Kirsty rushed after Amelie.
The goblins were squealing with fright.
They were all trying to climb up the mast
to escape from the water in the bottom of
the boat.

"Stay calm, and don't panic!" Amelie called down to them. She waved her wand over some thick, dark strands of seaweed floating on the waves. The magical fairy sparkles lifted the seaweed up and carried it over to the boat. As Rachel and Kirsty watched, the strands of seaweed plastered themselves against the hole in the side, quickly filling the gap.

"The boat stopped sinking," Rachel said, relieved.

"Follow me," Kirsty shouted to the three goblins. "I'll lead you through the rocks." She flew ahead, and the goblins rowed their boat after her. Then Amelie, Rachel, and Kirsty took the rope the goblins tossed to them and tethered the boat to one of the biggest rocks.

"Avast, my hearties, land ahoy!" the goblin in the bandanna proclaimed.

The goblin with the eye patch scowled. "*You're* not the captain of this ship," he complained, "*I* am!"

"I'm a better pirate than either of you," the third goblin said loudly.

"A 'thank you' would be nice!" Rachel murmured as the goblins ignored them and continued to argue.

"Let's leave them to figure it out," Amelie said with a grin, "and get back to our walrus!"

The three friends flew back the way they'd come. They were just in time to see the walrus lumber off across the rocks.

"Great!" Kirsty beamed, as she swooped down to where the walrus had been lying. "All we have to do now is pick up the piece of shell!" Her face fell as she scanned the rocks just below her. "But where *is* it?"

Rachel and Amelie flew down to look, too. But there was no sign of the shell piece.

"It's gone!" Rachel groaned.

Suddenly they heard a shout from one of the goblins. "After him! He has part of the golden conch shell!"

Rachel, Kirsty, and Amelie all turned to look. They saw the goblins running across the rocks, chasing after a little white seal pup. The pup had something golden and shiny in his mouth!

"That seal pup must have picked up the shell after the walrus moved!" Amelie cried. "Come on, girls!"

Amelie, Rachel, and Kirsty soared through the air toward the goblins and the seal pup. The goblin in the bandanna made a grab for the little pup, but at the last second his bandanna slipped right down over his eyes. He let out a shriek.

"Help! Where did the daylight go?"

The other two goblins shoved him out of the way and crept toward the seal pup.

He was now perched
on a rock,
watching
them with
big brown
eyes. They
leaped
forward
to capture
him, but
the pup
scooted away.

Immediately, Amelie, Rachel, and
Kirsty flew down and hovered around the
seal pup's head.

"Hello," Amelie said gently, "What's
that you have in your mouth? It looks
beautiful."

The pup watched quietly as Amelie

floated down to his level.
But then, looking
mischievous,
he ducked
aside and
rushed off.

"He thinks it's a game!"
Kirsty exclaimed as the pup let
the goblins get close to him before
dashing off again.

"Pesky fairies!" the goblin in the pirate
hat shouted, shaking his fist at them. "Go
away! The shell's ours!"

The seal pup had stopped a short
distance away and was watching Amelie,
the girls, and the goblin in the pirate hat.
Suddenly, Rachel noticed that the other
two goblins were silently creeping up
behind the pup.

"Look out!" Rachel called.

But it was too late. The two goblins pounced on the pup and held him down. The third goblin rushed over to them with a cry of triumph. The three of them began trying to pry the shell from the seal pup's mouth—but the pup refused to let go.

"Leave him alone!" Amelie called, but the goblins ignored her. Picking up the pup, they began carrying him across the rocks to their boat.

"Oh, no!" Rachel yelled. "The goblins are kidnapping the seal pup!"

The pup yelped loudly, and all the seals on the rocks turned their heads curiously to see what was happening. Before anyone could do anything, the goblins jumped into their boat, untied the rope, and set sail.

"What now?" Kirsty asked, looking upset as Silky and the other seals gathered around them. "The goblin has the seal pup *and* the shell!"

"Yes," Rachel agreed. "But we have something better."

"What?" asked Amelie.

"Just look around you," Rachel replied, as the goblins began to row as fast as they could away from the rocks. "We have lots of seals to help us! I'm sure Silky and the others can stop the goblins' boat!"

Amelie's face lit up. "Great idea, Rachel!" she declared. The fairy turned to Silky. "Silky, it's up to you and your friends! Can you rescue the seal pup and bring the piece of the golden conch shell back to us?"

Silky nodded his sleek head. He

barked a few times at the other seals on the rocks, and then all of them slipped silently and smoothly into the water. The goblins were so intent on making their escape, they didn't notice the seals swimming in their direction.

"Hey!" the goblin wearing the eye patch shouted nervously as Silky knocked against the boat, making it rock from side to side. "Who did that?" He glared at the other two goblins. "Was it you?"

The other goblins scowled back at him. Then all three of them yelled with fear as more of the seals began to bump and rock the boat!

"We're surrounded by sea monsters!" the goblin in the bandanna moaned, as he clutched the seal pup. "Somebody help us!"

Amelie, Rachel, and Kirsty flew across the waves toward them.

"We'll help you," Amelie called. "But only if you let the seal pup and the magic shell go!" Rachel and Kirsty waited, holding their breath. They looked at the little seal pup, still holding the piece of shell in its mouth. Would the goblins agree to do what Amelie asked?

Picture Perfect

"Never!" the goblins yelled.

Then they all let out frightened shouts as a group of seals dived under the water and began swimming underneath their boat, lifting it up in the air.

"We'll let him go! We'll let him go!" the goblins cried, gripping the boat and looking scared. The goblin holding the

seal pup lowered him into the ocean,
and the little seal swam happily over to
join his friends. He still held the piece of
golden conch shell in his mouth. Seeing
that he'd safely reached shore, the rest of
the seals headed back to land as well.

"This is a disaster!" the goblin in the
pirate hat shouted. "If
you two hadn't been
so scared, we wouldn't
have lost that piece
of shell!"
"You were
the most scared
of any of us!" the
goblin with the eye
patch replied. "You're a silly coward!"

"I am not!" the first goblin declared
furiously, jumping up and down in a rage.

"I'm going to be the captain now because I'm braver than you all," the other goblin announced. The boat began to rock and dip again as the three goblins argued with each other.

"Be careful," Amelie called, "or you'll wreck your boat again!"

Rachel and Kirsty laughed as the grumbling goblins sailed away. Meanwhile, the seal pup swam over to Silky and gave him the glittery shell piece. Silky barked a thank you and headed straight for Amelie, holding the

shell in his mouth. As he did, there was
a burst of golden sparkles, and Silky
shrank down to his tiny fairy size.

"Girls, we did it!" Amelie announced
happily, flying over to Silky. She gave
him a hug and took the shell from his
mouth. "We have our piece of the golden
conch shell at last. Will you come back
to Fairyland with me and give this to
Shannon?"

Rachel and Kirsty nodded eagerly.
Silky barked good-bye to his seal friends,
and the girls and Amelie waved at them.

"Thank you for all your help!" Amelie
called, waving her wand over herself,
Silky, Rachel, and Kirsty. They were
all transported back to Fairyland in a
swirling cloud of fairy magic!

When the fairy dust cleared, the girls saw that they were back in the Fairyland Royal Aquarium. Shannon and Ally were waiting for them, looking very excited. Silky was back in his glass tank next to Echo the dolphin, who was thrilled to see him. She swam happily around and around in circles, calling out a greeting.

"Good job!" Shannon declared. "It's wonderful to have you all back—and with another piece of the golden conch shell, too."

Amelie held out the shell piece to Shannon. Shannon took it and, cradling it carefully, she walked over to the table where the first piece of shell was waiting on a golden stand.

Rachel and Kirsty watched in amazement as the two pieces of shell sprang toward each other like magnets in a flash of golden light. They fitted together so neatly that, even though the girls studied them closely, they couldn't see any sign of a crack.

"You see?" Shannon said with a smile. "When we have all the pieces back, the golden conch shell will be as good as new! Thank you for your help, girls." She lifted her wand. "And now it's time to send you home."

"Good-bye," Rachel and Kirsty called, waving at Amelie, Silky, Echo, Ally, and Shannon. "We'll be looking out for the other Ocean Fairies!"

There was a whoosh of glittering fairy dust, and when Kirsty and Rachel opened their eyes again, they found themselves standing at the bottom of the spiral staircase inside the lighthouse.

"Oh, we're back!" Kirsty said. "Wasn't that a terrific fairy adventure, Rachel?"

Rachel nodded. "And now we know exactly how to make a walrus laugh!" she replied with a wink.

Smiling, the two girls left the lighthouse and went to find Kirsty's gran. They could see her still sitting at her easel, absorbed in her painting. But as they got closer, Rachel nudged Kirsty.

"Look at your gran's picture," she whispered.

Kirsty's eyes opened wide. Her gran had painted a group of seals playing on the rocky shore!

"Oh, hello, girls," Gran called as she dabbed some blue paint onto her canvas. "I wish you'd been here earlier. You won't believe it, but a pod of seals swam up Leamouth harbor and settled on the rocks over there. They were so beautiful!" Rachel and Kirsty shared a secret smile. They both knew exactly what the other was thinking: Which of the Ocean Fairies and their magical ocean creatures would they meet next?

THE OCEAN FAIRIES

Amelie the Seal Fairy has found
her piece of the golden conch shell!
Now Rachel and Kirsty must help

Pia

the Penguin Fairy!

Join their next underwater adventure
in this special sneak peek. . . .

Ice to
See You!

"*Wheeee!* This is fun!" squealed Kirsty
Tate as she sped along on roller skates.
"Beat you to that tree, Rachel!"

Kirsty's best friend, Rachel Walker,
grinned and picked up speed on her
skateboard. "I don't think so," she yelled
breathlessly, overtaking Kirsty at the last
moment. "I'm the winner!" she cheered,

slapping her hand on the trunk of the old oak tree a split second before Kirsty.

The two girls laughed. It was a sunny spring day and they were on vacation together at the seaside town of Leamouth. They were staying with Kirsty's gran for a whole week. Today they'd come to Leamouth Park, which overlooked the sea.

"Doesn't the water look pretty with the sun shining on it?" Kirsty commented dreamily, staring out at the ocean below them. It was a perfect blue.

"I know," Rachel agreed. "It's so sparkly, it almost looks magical." Then she grinned at Kirsty. "Speaking of magic, I hope we meet another Ocean Fairy today!"

"Me, too," Kirsty said.

Kirsty and Rachel started down the
path again. Before long, Kirsty heard
tinkling music drift over to them. "Is
that an ice-cream truck?" she asked
hopefully, feeling hungry at the thought.
Her gran had given them some spending
money, and suddenly it seemed like
breakfast had been a long time ago.

"Yes!" Rachel said, speeding farther
down the path and spotting the colorful
van parked near the playground. It was
still playing its cheerful tune and a large
plastic ice-cream cone rotated on the
roof of the van. "Come on, let's go over
and have a look."

The girls raced up to the van and
gazed at the pictures of ice cream on
the side. A friendly-looking man with a
white hat on his head leaned out of the

window. "What would you like, girls?" he asked.

"Creamsicle, ice-cream sandwich, chocolate dipped cone . . . Ooh, how are we going to choose?" Kirsty said, licking her lips as she read. "What are you getting, Rachel?" she asked.

Rachel didn't seem interested in the list of ice-cream at all. She was staring excitedly up at the roof of the van, where the plastic ice cream cone was still spinning.

As Kirsty gazed up at it, too, she realized why Rachel was so captivated. Perched on top of the revolving plastic cone sat a tiny smiling fairy, waving down at them. It was Pia the Penguin Fairy!

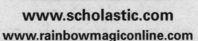

RAINBOW magic

These activities are magical!
Play dress-up, send friendship notes, and much more!

■SCHOLASTIC
www.scholastic.com
www.rainbowmagiconline.com

HiT entertainment

RMACTIVS